To our friend Richard

First U.S. edition 2016

Library of Congress Catalog Card Number pending

ISBN 978-0-7636-9251-3

16 17 18 19 20 21 LEO 10 9 8 7 6 5 4 3 2 1

Printed in Heshan, Guangdong, China

This book was typeset in WBHoráček.
The illustrations were done in mixed media.

Candlewick Press
99 Dover Street
Somerville, Massachusetts 02144

visit us at www.candlewick.com

BLUE
PENGUIN

Petr Horáček

CANDLEWICK PRESS

Far away, near the South Pole,
a blue penguin was born.

A blue penguin is not
something you see every day.

"Are you a real penguin?"
asked the other penguins.
"I feel like a penguin," said Blue Penguin.

Blue Penguin
did all the same
things that the
other penguins
did.

He wasn't the best at
diving or jumping,

but he always caught a big fish.
"I told you I was a penguin,"
said Blue Penguin.

"But you're not like us,"
said the other penguins,
and they wandered away.

Blue Penguin was left all alone.
His days were filled with emptiness.

His nights were filled with dreams.
There was one dream that came back
night after night. In this dream,
a beautiful white whale rescued
Blue Penguin, taking him away
from his lonely place.

Blue Penguin made up a song
about the white whale from his dream.
Each morning, he sang it across the ocean.
One day, a little penguin heard him singing.

Each day

she came a
little closer

to listen.

One day she spoke to Blue Penguin.
"Teach me your song," she said.

Each day, Blue Penguin taught
Little Penguin a bit more of the song,
and they sang and played together.
They became friends.

Then one evening Blue Penguin
turned to Little Penguin.
"It's time we sing a new song,"
he said. "I will teach you."

Blue Penguin's new song was so magical
that the other penguins came to listen.
When he had finished, they went up to him.
"Your song is beautiful," they said.
"Will you teach us to sing, too?"

"Yes," said Blue Penguin.
"Gather round and I will teach you."
But before they began to sing,
a huge white whale arrived.
"Who called me?" said the white whale.
"I heard my song and I have come."

Blue Penguin answered the white whale.
"It was I who called you. I dreamed of
you and wished you would come to
take me away from my loneliness."

Little Penguin looked sad.
"Don't leave," she said.
"You're my friend."

"Please don't leave us," said the other penguins. "We're sorry we left you alone. You're our friend as well. You're a penguin like us."

Blue Penguin looked at the white whale and said,
"Thank you for coming for me, but the song you heard
was a very old song. I have learned a new one now.
I belong here."

The white whale smiled, but said nothing. She turned
around and slowly disappeared over the horizon.

Blue Penguin turned to his friends.
"Now let us sing our new song,"
he said. "Our song of friendship."